Other *Young Puffin Read It Yourself* titles

DICK KING-SMITH

Huge Red Riding Hood

ILLUSTRATED BY
JOHN EASTWOOD

PUFFIN BOOKS

PUFFIN BOOKS

Published by the Penguin Group
Penguin Books Ltd, 27 Wrights Lane, London W8 5TZ, England
Penguin Putnam Inc., 375 Hudson Street, New York, New York 10014, USA
Penguin Books Australia Ltd, Ringwood, Victoria, Australia
Penguin Books Canada Ltd, 10 Alcorn Avenue, Toronto, Ontario, Canada M4V 3B2
Penguin Books (NZ) Ltd, Private Bag 102902, NSMC, Auckland, New Zealand

Penguin Books Ltd, Registered Offices: Harmondsworth, Middlesex, England

First published in *The Topsy-Turvy Storybook* by Victor Gollancz Ltd 1992
Published in Puffin Books 1998
5 7 9 10 8 6

Text copyright © Fox Busters Ltd, 1992
Illustrations copyright © John Eastwood, 1992, 1998
All rights reserved

The moral right of the author and illustrator has been asserted

Printed in Hong Kong by Wing King Tong

British Library Cataloguing in Publication Data
A CIP catalogue record for this book is available from the British Library

ISBN 0–141–30034–5

THE UGLY DUCKLING

An ordinary farmyard duck once hatched out a brood of ordinary ducklings. But when they were all free of their eggshells and scuttering about as newborn ducklings do, there was still one egg left in the nest.

It was a much bigger egg than the others had been, and the duck continued doggedly to sit upon it, hoping that it, too, would hatch. Which, some days later, it did.

Soon the duck could see that this last child was unlike his brothers and sisters. He was

larger, he was greyish where they were yellow, and his legs and feet were bigger and his neck much longer than theirs.

The duck thought him quite beautiful, and, proud mother that she was, she constantly told him so.

"You, my son," she said, day in, day out, "are beautiful. Your brothers and sisters are healthy normal ordinary ducklings, but you alone are beautiful," and she constantly showed him off to the other birds in the farm-yard, the hens and the geese and the turkeys.

"Look at him," the old duck said to them, day in, day out. "Is he not the most beautiful duckling you ever set eyes on?"

Not surprisingly, after all this constant flattery, the beautiful duckling grew up to be extremely big-headed.

He would stand by the duck pond and look at his reflection and say to himself, "Observe my noble body and my powerful wings and my great webbed feet and my long and elegant neck. What a truly beautiful duckling I am!"

And at last, to cap it all, his plumage which had been grey turned to a brilliant snowy whiteness.

One day the beautiful duckling left the duck pond and made his way to a nearby lake. Here he stood by the water's edge and looked once more at his reflection.

"Without doubt," he said, "I must be the most beautiful duckling in the world. No other could compare with me."

Then he looked up and saw a whole flock of great white birds swimming on the surface of the lake, birds that looked just like him, birds that certainly could compare with him.

"Even so, they cannot be as beautiful as I," he said to himself, and he swam proudly out to meet them.

At the sight of this stranger approaching
the swans banded together, arching their
wings and hissing angrily.

"Who are you?" they cried, and the reply
came "Make way! I am the beautiful duckling."

"Duckling!" said one of the swans to the
rest, and "He's mad!" said another. "And he's a
big-head!" said a third, and then a host of
voices said, "Let's duck the duckling!"

And with that all the swans set upon the
newcomer.

They buffeted him with their wings, and
pecked at him, and pulled out his tail feathers,

and finally they ducked his head under water.

Somehow, he struggled back to the duck pond, and saw the old duck who had hatched him so long ago but now did not recognize the battered, muddied bird, his neck limp, his wings trailing, his plumage all in dirty disarray.

"Who on earth are you?" she said.

"The beautiful duckling!" he gasped.

"A duckling you may be," said the old duck doubtfully, "but beautiful you are not. Sure as eggs is eggs, there's only one word to describe you. Ugly!"

POP GOES THE WEASEL

Half a pound of tuppenny rice,
Half a pound of treacle.
Finish off with five fat mice,
BURP! goes the weasel.

HUGE RED RIDING HOOD

There was once an enormous great lump of a girl called Huge Red Riding Hood. One day she set out to visit her grandmother, who lived alone in a little cottage in the woods.

Huge Red Riding Hood was carrying a basket of goodies for the old lady, but somehow before long the basket was empty. Huge Red Riding Hood rubbed her huge stomach.

"That's better!" she said.

Just then a wolf appeared and gazed at her hungrily. He thought of saying "Hello, little girl", but she obviously wasn't so he said, "Hello, huge girl" instead.

"Hi," said Huge Red Riding Hood, wiping her mouth on the back of her hand.

"And where are you going?" said the wolf.

"To visit my grandmother."

"And where does she live?" asked the wolf.

I'll get there first, he thought, and gobble

the old lady up. Then I'll get into bed and
pretend to be her and when this huge girl turns
up I'll have her for afters.

But Huge Red Riding Hood knew what he
was thinking, and she directed him to her grandmother's cottage by a long, roundabout route.
Then she took a short cut and got there first.

"Hello, dear," said her grandmother. "I see
you've brought me a basket of goodies."

"Don't worry about that, Gran," said Huge
Red Riding Hood. "There's a wolf on his way."

"But I'm hungry."

"So's he," said Huge Red Riding Hood. "You
get in the cupboard and keep quiet," and she
shoved the old lady inside and locked the
cupboard door.

Then she leapt into the bed and
pulled the covers over her head.

In a moment or two there was a
rat-tat on the front door and in came
the wolf. Immediately he sprang upon

the bed, intent on gobbling up the shape that he could see beneath the bedclothes.

As he did so, Huge Red Riding Hood suddenly exploded from beneath them and wrapped them all around the wolf – eiderdown and blankets and sheets – until he was completely enveloped.

Then Huge Red Riding Hood sat on him.

"Hey, wait a minute!" cried the wolf indistinctly from inside the bedclothes. "This isn't what's meant to happen. You should be saying, 'What big eyes you have and what big ears you have and what big teeth you have' and all that stuff. And anyway I can't breathe in here."

Feebly he cried "Let me out! Let me out!" but his voice grew weaker and weaker, until at last he suffocated.

Huge Red Riding Hood got off the heap of bedclothes and unwrapped them and pulled out the dead wolf by the tail. Then she dumped him outside in the garden.

"It's OK, Gran," she said, unlocking the door of the cupboard. "You can come out now."

But when her grandmother came out of the cupboard, all she said was, "What have you been doing with my bed? What an awful mess it's in!"

Then she looked in the basket that her granddaughter had brought.

"It's empty!" she cried. "You horrible child! You lock me in a cupboard, you make a filthy mess of my bed, and to top it all, you've wolfed all the goodies in the basket! What a way to treat your poor old granny! I never want to see you again. Get out!"

Huge Red Riding Hood got out. As she went down the garden path, she gently prodded the body of the wolf with her huge foot.

"Sorry, old chap," said Huge Red Riding Hood. "I should have let you eat her."

JACK SPRAT

Jack Sprat would eat no fat,
His wife would eat no lean,
So both turned vegetarian
And lived on peas and beans.

LITTLE JACK HORNER

Little Jack Horner
Sat in a corner,
Wolfing his Christmas pud;
Then he bolted his brother's,
His dad's and his mother's,
And said "I'm not feeling so good."

THE PRINCESS AND THE P
(FOR PUMPKIN)

There was once a Prince who wanted to get married. However, being a bit of a snob, he only wanted to marry a Princess. He travelled the world looking for a suitable one, but all the Princesses he met were such wimps, so precious and delicate, so *sensitive*.

"A namby-pamby lot they were, Mum," he said to the Queen on his return home. "I want a girl who can stand up for herself, a girl who can take the rough with the smooth."

"Maybe you'd better marry a commoner then," said the Queen.

"Not on your life," said the Prince.

Just then a great storm broke, and through the noise of the thunder they could hear someone banging on the palace doors.

The King went to open them, and in came a soaking wet girl.

"Jolly weather!" she cried with a merry laugh, and she shook herself like a dog, spattering them all with water.

She was a big strong handsome girl, the Prince could see.

"Are you," he said, "by any chance a Princess?"

"As a matter of fact I am," she replied, "and a jolly wet one at that."

"You'll catch your death of cold," said the Queen. "You'd better stay the night. I'll make up a bed for you."

She looks the right kind of girl, she said to herself, but we'd better find out how *sensitive* she is.

So she took all the clothes off the bed in the guest room, and then she put a pea on the bare bedstead. On top of the pea she put several mattresses and quilts, and on top of all that lot the Princess (after a nice hot bath) went to bed.

Later the Queen sneaked in to have a look but the Princess was fast asleep. So the Queen took out the pea and slipped in a lemon.

Several times more the Queen came back but each time the Princess was snoring her head off, while the Queen kept changing what was underneath all the mattresses and the quilts. She changed the lemon for a grapefruit and the grapefruit for a melon and the melon for a vegetable marrow. Finally the Queen staggered in with the largest pumpkin she could find. An enormous pumpkin it was, that anyone who was in the very least *sensitive* would have felt beneath her, no matter how many mattresses and quilts covered it, but it made no difference.

"One thing's sure, my boy," she said to the Prince at breakfast next morning. "This Princess is not a wimp, not precious or delicate, not in the very slightest bit *sensitive*. She's got a hide as thick as a rhinoceros."

Just then the Princess appeared.

"How did you sleep?" asked the Queen.

"Like a log," said the Princess.

"Want some breakfast?" said the King.

"I could eat a horse," said the Princess.

"Care to marry me?" said the Prince.

"Smashing idea!" cried the Princess, and she gave the Prince such a hearty slap on the back that his eyes filled with tears.

"Bless him!" she said to the King and the Queen. "He's so *sensitive!*"

PAT-A-CAKE

Pat-a-cake, pat-a-cake, baker's man,
Bake me a cake as rich as you can;
Ice it and slice it and serve it up hot,
And don't you tell Tommy 'cos I want the lot.

HANSEL AND GRETEL

Once there were two children, brother and sister, and very unlucky children they were.

First, they had a perfectly horrible mother and a weak wimpish father.

Second, there was a terrible famine in the land so that no one had enough to eat.

And third, their horrible mother said to her husband, "We can't feed four mouths, but we might still be able to feed two. Let's get rid of the kids," and their father was too weak and wimpish to say no.

So Hansel and Gretel were dumped in the depths of a forest in the middle of winter, and left to die – of cold and starvation.

Tragic, eh? Imagine the poor mites, lying in the snow, clasped in each other's little arms, waiting for Death.

Forget it. Hansel and Gretel were made of sterner stuff.

Disregarding the bitter cold, they set off hand in hand through the forest, not after their parents – they'd had enough of them – but in the opposite direction, and before long they came upon a dear little cottage among the trees.

Hurrying nearer, they found that the cottage was made, not of bricks and mortar, but, would you believe it, of bread and cakes, with windows of sugar.

They did not know that inside this cottage lived a sweet old white-haired apple-cheeked lady who was actually a wicked witch.

She had the most horrible habit. She ate children.

Hansel and Gretel, being terribly hungry, set about eating bits of the cottage.

Hansel had pulled off a piece of the roof and Gretel had smashed a window when out came the witch.

"Ha! Ha!" she cackled. "You're just in time for my evening meal."

"Oh good!" they said. "We're starving. What's for supper?"

"You are," said the witch. "The oven's nice and hot, all ready for you."

Hansel and Gretel looked at one another.

"I think she's a caliban," said Hansel.

"What's that?" said Gretel.

"Someone who eats people."

"Raw?"

"No, cooked."

"Oh," said Gretel. "Why do calibans eat people?"

"Because they're hungry."

"Oh," said Gretel. "We're hungry."

Hansel looked admiringly at his little sister.

"Gretel," he said, "you aren't just a pretty

face. Come on!" and between them the children dragged the wicked witch inside, and smeared her all over with lard, and shoved her in her own oven.

Later, when they'd eaten as much witch as they could manage and put the rest out in the snow to keep, they polished off the cottage for afters.

SIMPLE SIMON

Simple Simon met a pieman
Going to the fair.
Cried Simon "Hi! I want a pie!"
The pieman said "Beware!
"These pies cost three pounds each, you see.
"That's well beyond your range."
Said Simon "I've a nice new fiver –
"You can keep the change."

HUMPTY DUMPTY

Upon a rather wobbly wall
Fat Humpty Dumpty sat;
It couldn't bear his weight at all
And so it fell down flat.
The soldiers riding by could see
That Humpty wasn't spoiled.
"It didn't hurt a bit," said he,
For Humpty was hard-boiled.

JACK AND JILL

Jack and Jill
Went up the hill
To fetch a pail of water.
Said Jack "I'm hot,
"I'll drink the lot."
Said Jill "You didn't oughter.
"'Twill make you ill,
You'll catch a chill."
Said Jack "You make me tired."
But Jill was right.
That very night
Her brother Jack expired.